About the Author

Late in my life, at the age of seventy-two, I discovered that I like storytelling, I wanted to help children understand something about life after death, a word I don't like using as I know life is eternal. My main objective is to get children to think, WHAT IF, also to realize that there is more to life than just our existence on Earth. My wife and I live in Southern Tasmania, it is tranquil and peaceful, something we should all be seeking. There are five books in the Ugo and Jack series, please enjoy them.

Ugo and Jack Book 4

Geoff Parton

Ugo and Jack Book 4

Olympia Publishers
London

www.olympiapublishers.com

BUMBLEBEE PAPERBACK EDITION

A CIP catalogue record for this title is
available from the British Library.

ISBN: 978-1-83934-404-6

Bumblebee Books is an imprint of
Olympia Publishers.

First Published in 2022

Bumblebee Books
Tallis House
2 Tallis Street
London
EC4Y 0AB

Printed in Great Britain

Dedication

I dedicate this book to the children of the world.

Acknowledgements

Thank you to my wife, Jayne, for all her patience and help.

CHAPTER 1

That afternoon was spent in idle chitchat and a stroll in the garden with Eli, he seemed very nice, well-spoken and well-dressed in his immaculate uniform. Father was also impressed with him, however, Eli was going to sea, and it would be another six months before Elizabeth would see him again.

Some weeks passed before Ugo and Jack finally appeared to Elizabeth again, when she was preparing for bed one night. There was an array of sparkling lights; Elizabeth's hair blew back a little. A moment later, THE DOOR appeared, and through the opening stepped both Ugo and Jack. "Where have you two been," asked Elizabeth, "I have been waiting for you to explain to me what I'm doing here?" Ugo looked at her and said, "I see you've become accustomed to being called Elizabeth?"

"Yes," she answered, "that is the only name I have heard since I've been here, no one knows that my name is really Andi."

"Never mind," said Ugo chuckling to himself.

Andi asked again, "What's going on?"

Ugo started to speak, "Some time ago as you already know, Elizabeth went missing, she had an accident, her body was damaged to such an extent she was unable to be saved and so, ended up in the transit world rather than the spirit world."

He went on, "She has been there waiting for over two hundred years in your time but," he chuckled to himself, "it has only been a very short time for her. Originally, she came to the material world for a very special reason but was taken before she could complete her task. You, Andi, are now going to complete Elizabeth's task for her. The fact is, you have already started to take on Elizabeth's character and her memories... Elizabeth is still in the transit world although in spirit form only, she will be working with you and assisting you. In effect you will become her, the transition has already begun."

Andi just listened, and then, looking at Jack in an accusing way she said, "Did you know about this Uncle Jack?"

"I had an inkling, but didn't know all the details," Jack responded, "I thought that we came to the 1700s to prevent the fire in the warehouse, but that, as I know now, was only part of the reason. As I explained to you before, you are now a light being, this is what we do in the transit world. You will be given chores to do from time to time this is just one of many to come."

Then Ugo spoke again, "You will enjoy it here ...Elizabeth, as I will be calling you from now on, you will be treated very well, in fact you will live a life of luxury; both Jack and I will be here always for you if you need anything and if you have any questions. You will be able to see if you choose, how Andi is going from time to time."

Ugo also knew that Elizabeth would start to forget her previous life as time went by, he again chuckled using the word time then continued... "You see, Elizabeth, Andi is continuing Andi's life, and you are now continuing Elizabeth's life. You should start to acknowledge your new family by calling Mr Mont Grove your father, he would really love that; however, you must never mention anything that I have just told you about the real Elizabeth to anyone."

Andi just stood there with her mouth open, thinking to herself how strange all this was and how she felt that she had been divided into two; but she had learned that Ugo was always right.

Over the next month or two, Andi became quite used to being called Elizabeth, she didn't seem to miss her original home, as there were so many more new things to do here. She quite liked being waited on and wearing beautiful clothes. In general, she was treated like a princess. Sitting on the end of her bed, she started to think about last week's birthday party that her father had organised. It had been a large gathering of about a hundred people that she didn't know, but they all seemed to know her, they were all very friendly and courteous to her.

Father had hired a marquee which had been set up on the front lawn, there had been many tables laden with fresh salads, seafoods and other exotic dishes…

No expense had been spared, beautiful fine crockery and solid silver cutlery, it had been a grand event where everybody wore their best clothes.

A small orchestra had been set up in the ornate gazebo which stood central in the lawn area. They had played very old-fashioned music, Elizabeth thought to herself, but it had all been beautiful.

Apart from the well-dressed young ladies, there were also many young gentlemen wearing their top hats, long coats with tales, and fluffy white shirts. They all wore shiny boots with enormous buckles!

Most had arrived in private carriages with their own coachmen. It had been a grand celebration she would never forget, also due to the fact that everybody seemed delighted that I, Elizabeth, had returned home… She lay back on her bed thinking how lucky she was and wondering what was to be her task?

CHAPTER 2

Back at the old farmhouse, Andi seemed to have recovered from losing her uncle Jack but didn't feel very content as she still felt she needed to know more.

One day she enquired, "Mum, when Uncle Jack passed, I remember you said he would be with Ugo now, how do you know that?" Her mother's face flushed a little as she answered…

"Your Uncle is a great friend of Ugo's, he always said they would be together when he left. He knew lots of things about Fire Fly Valley and Ugo."

"Have you ever been there Mum?" asked Andi. Andi's mum didn't know quite how to answer, there were many things that she had not told Andi. But Andi was persistent, and eventually her mum answered, "Yes, I have been to Fire Fly Valley."

From that moment on, Andi bombarded her mum with questions like how did you get there, why did you go there, when did this all happen? 'I think it's time to tell Andi a bit about her past,' she thought to herself, thinking about how she should answer., she continued…

"When your uncle Jack was a young boy, he had an accident while swimming at the rock pool back on the farm. He hit his head and fell unconscious, while he was unconscious, he found he had moved into the transit world, or Fire Fly Valley, that's where he met Ugo.

Ugo explained to Jack, that Jack was a light being, and they were very old friends. During the course of his stay in Fire Fly Valley, Ugo realised that his old friend, Jack, was not happy, so adjustments were made to Jack's family, which by the way, hadn't been very harmonious for Jack or his brothers. The adjustments meant that Jack could return to a happy family life back on the farm, I will call Jack's family where he lived family one. However, there were members in the family that still had to experience certain things in their lives, which meant they were unable to stay with Jack's new family.

This left the family, where no adjustments had been made, to carry on living out their lives…I will call them family two." Andi's mom continued carefully…

"There are many different dimensions where humans live, some people call them parallel universes, but that is not really correct, they are simply people living out their lives where they can experience different circumstances… For example, Jack's brother John had to experience the hardships of alcoholism, and the loss of his daughter. Ugo decided to divide the families into two, so that all members were able to experience what they came to earth to do. Ugo knew Jack was a light being who had other reasons for being there, so he couldn't see the point of him struggling unnecessarily. I know it sounds complicated but look at it like this; if you were born into a rich family, you would be experiencing the riches of that life. On the other hand, if you were born into a poor family, you would experience poverty. There are many different dimensions living side-by-side, they're all separated a little except for the light beings and the Ugo's, nobody in the physical world knows they exist! In a way, there were two families living at the same time and place, however their lives turned out to be very different. In family one, Jack, Billy and John, the eldest brother, lived happily at the farmhouse. Unknowingly to Jack's brothers, because Jack was a light being, he was able to visit family two, where his older brother John also lived in the same farmhouse, but in a slightly different dimension. Jack was able to help Wilbur and Frederick when they ran into a little bit of trouble — it was a long time ago." She continued…

"Your Uncle Jack in a way is my uncle, when I say in a way, it's because your Uncle Jack, while living in family one, still had his brother John, who lived in family two as well as family one. Jack was able to see what was happening in family two, as he had the ability to move between the two dimensions…

In family two, John, Jack's eldest brother, was married and had three children who were Wilbur, Frederick and Rebecca."

"That's your name, Mum!" Andi exclaimed.

"Yes, I know," replied Rebecca. Andi then enquired, "I thought Wilbur and Frederick's sister; drowned when she was a little girl?"

"Yes, that's correct Andi." Andi just looked at her mum and questioned, "I still don't understand."

Andi's mum went on. "Well, it's like this, Rebecca did drown, but went to Fire Fly Valley where she also met Ugo. Ugo explained to her that she had to return to complete certain tasks here."

"How do you know all this?" Asked Andi.

"Because, I am the same Rebecca!"

She went on to explain to Andi, that quite a few members of the family are in fact light beings, although some of them are not even aware of it. "There are many things that you don't know Andi. Uncle Jack is a light being, he also knew about the two parallel families. From time to time, he visited family two in order to help them out. Your Uncle Jack is a very wise man, or should I say, spirit man, as he is now living back in Fire Fly Valley. I have no doubt he is traveling around doing all sorts of other things to help people."

Andi just sat and listened, and started to wonder… "Who am I Mum?" She asked, "am I normal, or do I have a parallel family as well?"

Rebecca thought for a moment, 'should I answer her and tell her about Elizabeth? — No, not yet anyway.'

"That's enough for today," Rebecca stated, "and you have homework to do." Andi went up to her room thinking homework, homework, always homework!

Then, from out of the blue, Ugo appeared in Rebecca's kitchen.

Rebecca looked up with a slightly surprised look on her

face. "Hello Ugo, it's so good to see you again."

Ugo was standing there, tall and bottle like, semi-transparent with no arms, big eyes and that beautiful big loving smile. He came closer to Rebecca and surrounded her in his bubble of love.

While Andi was doing her homework, both Ugo and Rebecca drifted out into the garden, and for the moment — into timelessness, where they sat and talked.

Ugo explained to Rebecca, that he felt she had spoken to Andi about certain things, and asked...

"You haven't told her too much have you? You haven't mentioned Elizabeth to her yet have you?"

"No, no, I don't think she is ready to fully understand it yet anyhow," she replied.

"Good." Ugo said, "Elizabeth is doing very well in her new role, she has taken on most of Elizabeth's original character, and hardly ever refers to things back here."

"Tell me, how far should I go, and when should I tell Andi the rest?"

"I think you have told her enough for now, I wouldn't tell her any more until she asks, and she will; your daughter is very inquisitive. I must be going back to Fire Fly Valley now, there are other lives I have to deal with." Ugo laughed to himself.

Then he gave Rebecca an invisible cuddle before departing through the opened crackling DOOR, which led to Fire Fly Valley.

The next day, as Andi and Rebecca were having breakfast Andi asked, "Does Uncle Frederick and Uncle Wilbur know that you returned?" Rebecca thought to herself, 'oh dear,' then she answered... "No, they don't know. They think that I was drowned when I was a child and that was that. They must never know — that's why you have never seen them, and I have kept them out of your life." She finished.

Andi thought about that and asked, "does that mean you are a light being also, and if so, what am I?"

"Yes, that's correct I am and so are you! But we have to keep all this our little secret; We live in an unusual family, but we have been blessed that we know that dying is only a transition from this world to the next; as Ugo has stated many times — nothing ever dies."

"Mum." Andi persisted, "how come I'm a light being?"

"Because you are the daughter of a light being, which is me!"

CHAPTER 3

One day Ugo was speaking with Jack, and said, "I would like to return to Mont Grove estate, to see how Elizabeth and Eli are doing."

"Who's Eli?" Jack asked in amazement.

"Eli, is the young man that Elizabeth met when she first arrived at the manner, he was in the navy — and still is. They fell in love instantly and were married two years later." Ugo explained.

"Going back sounds like a great idea... I often wonder how she's adapting." Jack said.

Ugo chuckled out loud...

"What's so funny?" Jack asked.

Ugo continued, "isn't it a wonderful thing to be able to move around in so called time? We are going to go back at the turn of the century, the year will be 1800, or page 1800 in the great book of life. There are great things happening, many celebrations as all the people are seeing in, a new century — the year is 1800."

"Wait a minute," Jack proclaimed, "we were there

just the other day! Elizabeth was about to turn seventeen, that was 1786."

Ugo chuckled again and explained. "When we see Elizabeth next, she will be thirty-one, she's married and has two children, so let's go back and see how things are?"

Ugo and Jack dressed for the occasion, they wore 1800s' clothes, looking like two well off citizens of the day. THE DOOR appeared, and as planned they stepped through. A moment later, they appeared in the gardens at the Mont Grove estate. There where hundreds of guests celebrating the New Year. Everybody appeared happy and cheering, it was a major event in the great book of life. It was the turn of the century and Fireworks were going off everywhere — as a result nobody noticed THE DOOR sparkling and crackling as it opened into the garden.

Both Ugo and Jack were enjoying the festival atmosphere, when Jack thought he spotted Andi, or rather Elizabeth.

"Goodness me!" Jack exclaimed to Ugo, "is that Elizabeth? Look at her, she's grown into a beautiful woman, and that must be Eli beside her."

"Yes," said Ugo, 'the perfect couple,' he thought to himself.

Elizabeth hadn't noticed Ugo and Jack standing there, she was far too occupied calling to her two boys. Jack in particular was taken aback when two well-dressed excited young boys ran over to their mum and dad. Eli was heard saying... "Come on boys, come on — we have to go in now it's bedtime for you."

Both Jack and Ugo just stood there watching as

Elizabeth, Eli and their two boys strolled back towards the manner. Elizabeth had a strange feeling as she walked toward the manor, she glanced back but noticed nothing.

Both Ugo and Jack wanted to meet with Elizabeth but had to choose the time carefully as neither Eli nor the boys knew anything about Elizabeth, the fact that she was a light being. And that Elizabeth had to be kept secret — here at the manner. Elizabeth's father also had no idea that Elizabeth had been Andi from a future time.

The next day after lunch, Elizabeth decided to take a walk in the garden on her own. Ugo and Jack thought this was the right time to appear. Elizabeth had walked quite a long way through the gardens and was now sitting on a garden seat, one of her favourite spots under a giant oak tree.

As she sat there. she quietly thought about all the different events that were going to happen in the 1800's, and how no matter what, she knew she could not interfere with anything. As far as she was concerned, so-called future events she knew had already taken place, were still to come for everybody that was living in the 1800's.

Then out of the blue, a flash of lights, then a crackling sound, a slight breeze arose, instantly in front of her THE DOOR appeared!

Even though she recognised it, she was momentarily startled as she hadn't seen it for so many years. Through the door stepped Ugo and Jack — Elizabeth's face lit up as she exclaimed, "Oh it's you Uncle Jack and Ugo, I haven't seen you both for so long, where have you been?" Ugo and Jack approached Elizabeth, and for some moments all three were encompassed in a beautiful bubble of love. No one said anything, they just stood there enjoying the wonderful feeling. Elizabeth was first to step back saying. "I have missed you both so much, such a lot has happened here, I didn't think I'd ever see you again it's been so long." The words came tumbling out of Elizabeth mouth, as she was overcome with excitement and questions.

Uncle Jack spoke first saying. "I can hardly believe how much you have changed, when I saw you last you were a sixteen-year-old young lady, now look at you, you are a beautiful woman with two wonderful boys."

"Yes," Elizabeth answered, "they are twins, they are eleven and will turn twelve in about six months' time. Have you seen my husband, Eli? He's a wonderful man and a wonderful father. I have been blessed."

Both Ugo and Jack spoke almost at the same time… "We would love to meet Eli, but he can't know of our existence at this stage. If your father finds out that you are not who you say you are, he will be severely hurt, your secret must stay secret."

Elizabeth then asked, "Why did I come here, what was my task that was so important?"

Ugo answered. "You have already accomplished your task, just enjoy your lovely life of luxury!"

"What was my task?" Elizabeth persisted.

Ugo replied. "It's the boys, you had to give birth to two boys, that was your task. They are here now; their part in the coming future is of great importance to the world. We will guide them and protect them." Elizabeth queried, "but they are only eleven, it will be another ten

24

years before they are adults!"

"As you know..." Ugo went on, "time is meaningless. For us, ten years can be gone in a blink." He chuckled, "do you remember how we moved forward in time when you were captive on the ship?"

Elizabeth thought about this for a while; just for a moment she was there on the ship, cannons roaring, the strong smell of gunpowder. Returning to the moment she said, "yes, I remember now." It had been a long time ago, then she remembered Andi and asked...

"Tell me, how is Andi?"

"Andi is fine, she has been told all about her mother," replied Ugo.

"You mean she knows about me being here, and that her mother is a light being?"

"Yes Elizabeth, although Andi has never been to Fire Fly Valley — Jack has told her all about it."

'It was strange,' Elizabeth thought to herself, 'how Andi now seemed almost like a dream from the past, or should I say the future.' she thought to herself, my real life is here now at Mont Grove estate.

"What are your two boys' names?" Jack asked.

"I have named them William and Henry."

Jack went on, "which ones which, they both look the same."

Elizabeth answered, "yes, they tricked me for quite some time as they are identical twins. They used to play jokes on me... I would call one and the other would come! But now I know which is which... William's ears are slightly different, his right ear is a little higher than his left, whereas Henry's ears are almost equal... well, that's how I tell them apart anyhow."

CHAPTER 4

Mont Grove estate was huge, it backed onto one of the biggest forests in the land, the boys often said they wanted to venture into the forest, but they weren't allowed, although they were never told why.

Henry and William had full use of the Estate's horses, they often talked about getting their own horses, although they hadn't had the courage to ask their father yet.

One evening, both boys went to their father and asked...

"Dad, when can we get our own horses to ride?" Eli glanced over at Elizabeth knowing she was listening and wondered what she was thinking. He said to her, "I suppose it's about time they had their own horses, what do you think dear?"

Elizabeth smiled a little, then Eli looked back to the boys and said, "I can't see why you can't have your own horses soon." The boys were very excited and wondered why they hadn't asked before.

Eli and Elizabeth discussed the matter that night after the boys had gone to bed, they decided that they would buy two horses from a neighbour who had a horse stud. The next day, Eli rode over to his neighbour Mr. Wells, who bred horses, and asked if he would like to sell a couple of horses for the boys... "It was time," he said, "for the boys to have some independence and responsibility."

Mr. Wells answered, "I have two beauties; I got them just last week, I think they would suit your boys perfectly."

Unknowingly to Mr. Wells and Eli — Bonnie and Bobby were very special horses, they had been sent from Fire Fly Valley by Ugo. An agreement was struck up between both parties, within an hour Eli was riding back to Mont Grove estate leading the two beautiful horses whose names were Bonnie and Bobby. Bobby was a dapple grey, Bonnie was a chestnut. When Eli returned to Mont Grove, he led the two horses directly to the stables where the stable boy had everything ready for them. Eli said nothing, he wanted it to be a surprise for the boys.

Next day after breakfast, Eli said to the boys, "come with me you two, I have something to show you both." Eli led the way as they walked to the stables, the two boys walked side-by-side. Eli opened the big stable door to the sound of horses snorting their horsey aroma wafted over them. All three walked down the stable corridor which had stables on either side. Eli then stopped and said to the boys, "look there." The boys turned and saw the two beautiful horses exclaiming...

"I've not seen these horses before Dad." William spoke first.

"Neither have I." Henry followed.

Eli looked at the boys and said with a slight smile on his face, "well, how do you like them?"

The boy's hearts were pumping with anticipation. "Yes, yes," they said, "they are very beautiful!"

"Then they are yours," said Eli.

"Which one do I get?" Henry asked eagerly, but before Eli could answer William said, "I like the grey one."

Then Henry said, "I like the chestnut."

"Good," said Eli, "then it's settled; William, you have the grey, Henry, you have the chestnut."

"Can we ride them now Dad?"

"Yes, but after lunch."

Lunchtime came and went, neither Henry nor William ate very much they were far too excited. Eli barely got his last mouthful down his neck when the boys started begging him saying, "come on, come on Dad, let's go riding?"

"All right, you boys go and get your breeches and boots on, I'll meet you at the stables."

The boys rushed upstairs to get changed, meanwhile Eli walked over to the stables to ask the stable boy to prepare the boys horses for riding. The stable boy was just leading the two horses out when Henry and William came running down to the stables, wearing their breeches and riding boots and caps.

The boys who were both good riders, took the reins

and swung up onto their saddles.

Eli called out… "Just walk the horses up and down here first boys, so I can watch how you are handling them."

The horses were lively and had obviously been well-trained. Eli thought — 'they seemed to respond instantly to the boys' movements of the reins.'

Both boys walked the horses up the driveway about 70 or 80 metres; Then Eli shouted, "take them for a little trot boys."

Both horses started to trot, then a second later the grey broke into a slow ambling canter, next thing the chestnut also was cantering. Eli could see that the boys had full control of them and saw no reason why they couldn't go for a ride by themselves. He called the boys back and told them that they could go for a ride if they wanted, but to be careful and make sure that they were home before the sun started to set.

With that, the two boys cantered off up over the small hill that lay in front of them. Eli watched the boys disappear over the crest of the hill in the distance, thinking to himself how wonderful it was seeing the two boys growing up and enjoying their lives.

Henry and William rode the horses around the massive estate, eventually the boys saw the edge of the dark forest not too far away, going to the forest was out of bounds, and they both knew it, but the temptation was still there.

They turned around and slowly let the horses walk back towards the manor. Riding side-by-side chatting away and feeling like grown-ups. William said to Henry, "one day I want to go into the forest!"

"But we're not allowed," said Henry shocked.

"I know, but I want to do it anyway," he replied to Henry.

"Yes, you are right, I'd like to take the chance too."

Then with just a little nudge of their heels, both horses broke into a canter, the boys were laughing happily as they cantered down through the thick grass and then onto the long driveway which led back to the manner and the stables. Arriving back at the stables, the stable boy took both horses and led them away to be brushed and fed.

The boys then ran to the main entrance like it was some sort of race, when they got to the door William said, "I beat you."

"No, you didn't, I got here first." Henry replied a little out of breath.

Elizabeth took one look at the boys and ordered... "Go upstairs boys and prepare yourself for a bath, I'll have Judy run one. Don't be long, dinner will be called soon."

That night, when the boys were lying in bed, they were talking to each other saying, "what are we going to call them, the horses?" William asked.

"I don't know, I'll think of a name tonight in my dreams, I just can't stop thinking about riding into the dark forest tomorrow, what it might be like." Henry replied.

They lay there wondering if there would be any wolves or deer in the forest. Their candles had burned out long ago, but they could still hear the sound of the piano downstairs being played softly by Elizabeth. That night when the boys fell asleep, they both dreamt about the horses, Ugo was present in their dream. The boys didn't know it, but they kept being told to call the horses Bobby and Bonnie!

CHAPTER 5

The next day straight after breakfast the boys asked if they could go riding. Eli answered... "So, you must have enjoyed your ride yesterday?"

"Oh yes, yes!" they said in tandem, "we want to go again now, and can we take something to eat and drink please, then we don't have to return for lunch?"

Eli looked at Elizabeth for a nod, which she gave. Eli looked back at the boys and said, "I'll have the kitchen maid make a picnic basket for you. In the meantime, go and get your breeches and boots on," he said with a smile.

The boys ran upstairs to their rooms to get changed. It wasn't long before they were setting off, but this time, they had a plan.

Dressed the same — grey breaches with their black shiny boots. They also both wore a red coat each, and a black cap. Anybody that may have seen them, would have been unable to tell one from the other, they looked identical.

They rode for about an hour, discussing as they went the new names that they had thought up for the horses. It was agreed upon that Bonnie and Bobby would be their new names. Of course, unknowingly, Ugo had planted the two names in the boys' memory from the previous night's dreams.

The forbidden forest appeared not too far away. Both boys stopped for a moment as they gazed at the mysterious darkness of the forest, they wondered why they had never been allowed to enter. There had been rumours of people entering the dark forest and never returning — perhaps that was why they were not allowed to go into the forest? Anyway, they agreed with each other, they were only rumours.

Walking their horses gently towards the forest, it appeared to get larger and larger as they approached. At the edge of the forest, they saw a single file track weaving between the trees. The horses became a little nervous and twitchy stamping their feet and snorting. Bonnie looked at Bobby and gave a little wink, they both knew what was in store for the two boys as they entered the mysterious forest.

"Let's not go too far in," Henry said.

"Don't be a scaredy cat, we can always turn around and go back out the same way." William responded authoritatively.

The boys decided that they may not get the chance again so started to walk the horses slowly into the eerie darkness. They followed the small walking track which seemed to beckon them on. Without saying anything to each other, they kept on following it single file, as it was so narrow.

William led the way on Bobby, his dapple-grey horse. Close behind was Henry on his chestnut mare, Bonnie. As they entered the forest, the darkness seemed to encompass them both, almost closing in behind them. The sun that had been quite bright outside, now struggled to filter through the thick canopy above them, allowing tiny streaks of light to penetrate through the tall trees.

"I don't like this much William, something's not right here."

William started to answer, but after hearing the first word that came out of his mouth he stopped, realising his voice was trembling, and not wanting to appear weak. So, he just turned slightly and beckoned Henry with his hand to keep following him.

They rode on for some time without talking — Henry in particular kept looking back at the little track just to make sure it was still there. The truth was, he felt like turning the horse around and galloping out of the forest but, knew he had to stay with William for protection and for his pride. They rode on for quite some time, eventually William said, "have you noticed Henry, it's becoming a bit brighter?"

"Yes, you're right."

Another 50 or 60 metres they appeared to be coming out of the forest. In front of them was a very large round clearing, they stopped at the edge for a moment. They thought to themselves how strange it all seemed. The clearing looked like a great big circle —

around the perimeter in all directions you could see the forest thickening up again, as it had been all the way so far. They decided to walk across the empty space where nothing seemed to be growing, to see if they could pick up the little track again on the other side of the clearing.

As they started to ride onto the clearing, a strange thing happened, the sound of the horses' hooves suddenly changed from a normal clip clop to a deep hollow resonating sound. Both boys looked at each other, then Henry spoke, "what's going on, can you hear the hooves William, they sound different."

"Yes," answered William.

"It's like a drumming noise," said Henry, "it sounds like it's hollow underneath us."

Instead of walking straight across the big desert like circle, they decided to just ride around on the cleared circle, to see if the sound of the hoofs changed, it did not.

Suspecting it was a great big cave underneath, they thought there should be an entrance somewhere. Then they decided it was time to investigate and see if it was really hollow or not. Dismounting, they tied the horses to one of the trees on the edge of the great circle, where there was a small amount of green grass to keep the horses occupied while they went off exploring.

Bonnie looked at Bobby and said quietly to the other, "have you seen Rrrr pronouncing his name like a growl? He should be here by now to help the boys."

Bobby answered, "Oh, he'll be here, he is reliable even if he is annoying sometimes."

"Henry," William called out, "you go that way, and

I'll go this way, and we'll meet somewhere around the other side, what do you think?"

Henry immediately said, "No, no, we should stick together in case something goes wrong." William agreed because that's what he really wanted but just didn't want to lose face. So, they both set off timidly to circumnavigate the huge empty space. Assuming it was hollow underneath, 'there must be an entrance,' they thought. The search was on looking for some type of opening, a doorway, or an entrance of some sort to what they thought must be an underground cave.

They decided to go in an anticlockwise direction keeping an eye on the clearing at all times, so if necessary, they could make a quick escape for the horses.

Clambering through the dense forest was not easy, but they did find what appeared to be the remnants of a very small old path which continually disappeared and then reappeared. As it was so overgrown, it was very difficult to follow. They clambered on for quite some time with very little change, certainly there was no sign of any entrance. William then spoke saying, "I think we are wasting our time, I don't think there's anything here that's too unusual,"

Henry on the other hand replied, "It sounded like it was hollow to me, I say let's keep looking."

The boys continued on for quite some time, they had been walking for at least an hour, but were only about two-thirds of the way around the circle. Then in front of them they came across a rocky outcrop, the scene changed dramatically, there were huge rocks which looked like they had been stacked on top of each other by some monster hand — it just looked artificial. They looked back behind them, something was very odd, a fog now surrounded them which made it impossible to see the little path that they had just traversed. There was only one direction to go, and that was straight ahead. Nothing could be heard, no sound whatsoever, it was a strange and scary feeling.

They clambered around the rocks seeing if they could find the little path once more, but it seemed to have disappeared totally! They continued on hoping eventually they would leave the rocky outcrop and get back into the forest again. All of a sudden Henry yelled out, "William, look, there's the little path again."

William turned around, they both went closer for a better look.

"Yes, it's the path, you're right Henry, look it's leading to the big rock face over there."

They both walked over to the rock face quickly, then stopped and looked at each other.

William spoke first. "It doesn't go anywhere, it just stops here at the rock!"

"That's strange," Henry replied, "the track just ends." As he said that, he leaned against the rock face placing his hand on the surface of the rock. Without warning, there was a crackling sound accompanied by a sudden breeze, then the whole rock face seemed to light up with coloured flashing lights surrounding what appeared to be an opening.

Both boys leapt back from the rock face, and as they

did, everything returned to normal again.

"What was that?" asked Henry frightened.

"I don't know," William responded, "I've never seen anything like these flashing coloured lights, and crackling noises!"

"Me either... and I think we should go home." Henry continued, "or maybe, you put your hand on the wall William, let's see what happens? That's if you're brave enough?"

The challenge was taken up as William walked forward and placed his hand firmly on the rock face, while using his other hand to steady himself. This time as William held his hand on the wall, without any warning the same thing happened again, lights flashed, a crackling sound was heard, followed by a slight breeze which blew the boys hair back a little. Then directly in front of them appeared some type of entrance, they could now see the little path continuing on through what appeared to be another forest, or was it, they weren't at all sure. What had moments before been a solid rock was now a misty hole or doorway, still surrounded by flashing lights beckoning them, almost calling to them saying "Come in, come in".

Without any thought, Henry took a step through with William directly behind him, two more steps and they found themselves in not just a forest, but another strange world.

William glanced behind him only to find the solid rock face had returned. Looking ahead again, he could still see the path continuing on... There was nowhere else to go but to follow the little path. "What is this place?" Queried William, "there's something very different here — something's not natural. Look over there, Henry, look at the size of those trees, they are so big we couldn't possibly be in a cave, or they'd be sticking out into the clearing...there's light from the sun, but where is the sun?"

"I can't see it," Henry replied.

Everything looked right but somehow nothing was right, the trees were too big, the river that ran through was shiny and twinkling, but far too big for a cave. There was a sense of life everywhere you could feel it, but they couldn't see anything, the grass seemed abnormally green. "Look," said Henry as he laid down and rolled in the grass, "it's soft like grand mamma's rug, it's beautiful, I love it."

CHAPTER 6

Bobby and Bonnie had both seen the flash from where they were tied up, they knew the boys must have been at THE DOOR, Bonnie said, "I hope Rrrr is there."

The boys just kept walking following the now very faint path when suddenly, there was a slight movement at the base of one of the large trees — both boys looked down, there they saw a small creature. It was like nothing they had ever seen before, it had two legs and two arms and a head, but didn't look like a boy, it was far too small. Its face was covered in wrinkles, and it had a cheeky mischievous look about it. Two very big ears like a donkey protruded from its head. When it laughed, it showed a row of what looked like dirty brown teeth and yet, it was cute in a way.

It was staring at both William and Henry and began to laugh. Then the boys where close enough to get a whiff of its bad breath.

"Do you like it here?" He asked. Before the boys had time to answer, he continued, "what are you going to do now? How are you going to get back through the rock wall? Ha, ha, ha — he, he, he." He laughed mischievously knowing he was in total control. "Who are you?" Henry asked.

"I am Rrrr" — it answered still laughing. Rrrr started to jump around, next thing it was on one of the branches of the trees, then it started moving around everywhere jumping from one tree to another, then onto a rock, the boys found it difficult to follow him.

"I'm over here," Rrrr said teasingly... Then, "I am over here," moving to yet another place.

"He is clearly playing games with us," William said, "and did you smell his breath? Phew! What are you doing here, and what is this place?" William asked rather annoyed.

Rrrr immediately answered with another question. "What are you two doing here?" Knowing that everything had been arranged by him.

Henry answered nervously, "we found an entrance in the rock, and we just came through it!"

"I know, I've been watching you, ha, ha, ha, ha." Rrrr laughed wickedly.

"Where are we, what is this place?" asked William again feeling a bit more annoyed?

Rrrr answered with yet another question. "Would you like to see more boys... I can show you lots of special things." He said with a devious look on his old, wrinkled face.

"Why are you called Rrrr? It sounds silly!"

Rrrr answered sheepishly, "It's not my real name... no,

no, no, — it's a nickname that the big fella gave me."

"Big fella! Who's the big fella?"

"The one with no arms!" He teased and laughed again.

"Rrrr's a very strange name," continued William, "what does it mean?"

Rrrr answered hesitantly, "he calls me Rrrr, because he thinks I'm a rotten rascal, that's what the R stands for you see."

"Are you a rotten rascal?" Henry asked, trying not to laugh.

"Of course, I'm not, just a good little nature spirit that likes a bit of fun from time to time." He turned his head slightly showing a sneaky grin, and went on, "you boys aren't supposed to come into the forest, they don't want you to find out about this place."

"What do you mean they, who's they, and what is there to find out about?"

"This place…you silly boys," he answered tormentingly, starting to laugh again.

"What is this place?" William asked yet again.

"You'll find out later, that is, if I let you go home, ha, ha, ha." Rrrr laughed as he jumped to another branch nearer the boys, a waft of bad breath hit them as he showed his dirty brown teeth.

Then Henry asked, "who is this big fella, the one you just mentioned?"

Rrrr replied, "he's the boss man, at least he thinks he is." Rrrr raised his eyebrows and continued, "you'll meet him one day."

Henry asked again, "why has he got no arms, was

there an accident?"

"No, no, no," Rrrr answered with frustration, "he's just a big walking bottle! He comes here sometimes, you're bound to see him, he's very friendly, he's always laughing too."

The boys realised all of a sudden, that they must have been there for quite some time, and that they should be returning back.

"It must be getting late," Henry said, "we should be returning, or we will be in trouble."

Rrrr just looked at them and said teasingly… "So, you want to go home do you? I suppose you want me to show you where the door is, Hmmm? I'll have to think about that." He stood there scratching his head as though he was undecided, then said, "Oh come on then, follow me."

Rrrr seemed to just drift along, following the same little path which moments before had not been visible. Both boys were also drifting but hadn't noticed it, they just followed him. The path seemed to lead straight towards the rock wall again.

Henry quietly said to William, "do you think he's going to let us out?" Before William had time to answer, Rrrr said quickly, "I can hear you! Everything you say I can hear — haven't you noticed the size of my ears?" He flicked one of them back and forth to get their attention.

They were almost at the rock wall when Rrrr looked back at them and winked, then he just seemed to drift straight into the rock. As he did so, the lights and the rush of wind and the crackling sound all happened at once. Next thing all three stepped back out into the rocky outcrop. Feeling much safer and braver, the boys quickly clambered up onto one of the big boulders to see if they could get a clear view of the clearing. Sure enough, not far away they saw their two horses — still tied to the tree happily nibbling on the grass.

Bonnie looked at Bobby, and said quietly to him, "look they're back."

The sun was shining high in the sky as it had been before. It felt like no time had passed — it was just as though none of this had happened because their two horses were still tied to the tree.

William called out to Henry, "where has that rascal gone now, is he following us?"

They both looked around but couldn't see him anywhere.

"I can't see him," Henry replied, "but nothing would surprise me." They walked to the horses noticing they had hardly eaten any grass. They mounted up for the long ride back home to the manner thinking — 'it must be getting late,' but the sun seemed to be in the same place as it was before… very strange!

Rrrr quickly jumped on the horse Bobbie, settling himself behind William who did not notice.

'May as well get a ride back,' he thought to himself. Bobbie's ears turned quickly as he showed the whites of his eyes in annoyance. 'How dare he? What a rascal!' he thought to himself.

They rode the horses back into the forest leaving the cleared circle behind. They followed in single file along the narrow track they had taken into the forest earlier.

It took some time, but eventually the forest started to thin out and the darkness caused by all the shadows, slowly disappeared.

Henry called excitedly to William, "look Will, I can see the open fields ahead."

The horses started to trot with anticipation — next thing they were out and free. Both boys began feeling very relieved, and yet, both were already thinking about their next visit.

The horses broke into a canter without being asked, then Bobbie gave a little buck in the hope that Rrrr might get tossed off his back! He heard Rrrr yell out. "Stop that Bobbie, I might fall off!" Bobby glanced back to see Rrrr hanging on and laughed to himself.

The boys where glad they were out in the sunshine and the grassy fields once more, as they headed back home to Mont Grove Estate.

On arrival at the stables, the boys passed the horses to the stable boy ignoring his comment about the horses being sweaty. They ran excitedly to the main door where the sound of their voices alerted the butler — the doors opened slowly as they approached.

Eli their father happened to be standing nearby, he asked, "did you boys have a good ride?"

"Oh yes," Henry answered, almost out of breath, "it was great," he was careful not to mention the forest of course.

"You haven't been gone very long; I thought maybe one of the horses had lost a shoe when I saw you coming back so soon." Neither of the boys were game to say that they had been to the forest — and certainly couldn't say anything about meeting Rrrr.

"No Dad," William said, "the horses looked a bit tired, so we decided to return early."

Eli responded, "I understand, that's good, boys, you'd better change out of those clothes as we're about to have lunch. By the way, did you have your picnic lunch?"

The boys just looked at each other, they had forgotten all about their lunch, and replied. "Ah, we forgot about the picnic lunch, sorry Dad." Eli frowned as he looked at them with a questioning look, thinking to himself, 'boys never forget to eat!'

CHAPTER 7

That evening the boys were far too excited to go to sleep, they couldn't stop talking about the day's events in the dark forest, and then meeting Rrrr, the rascal.

William spoke first saying, "I want to go back I want to see more Henry." Henry was a little frightened, but after some persuasion he agreed they should return.

"Dad doesn't know that we've been to the forest, if he finds out we will be in terrible trouble," Henry replied.

Then a little sly voice was heard, "don't tell him, mustn't tell him!" Both boys looked around to see where the voice had come from, there sitting on the windowsill was Rrrr who went on… "It's better to keep this a secret, boys, our little secret." His eyes flashed around the room suspicion on his face. One of his big ears flicked around as though checking for anyone who might be listening, then continued. "You're not doing anything wrong boys, I can show you all sorts of things," he taunted. With that he jumped out of the window and disappeared. The boys looked at each other and thought to themselves, 'that was the rotten rascal.'

"What's he doing here in our bedroom?" Henry speculated, "and how does he know where we live?"

"He must've followed us here," whispered William, "anyhow, we will ride out to the dark forest as soon as we can, then we'll find out, what do you think Henry?" as he looked over at Henry who nodded in approval.

It was almost a week later before the boys were able to get away on their horses. They had on their riding breaches and red jackets, then saddled up the horses to discreetly head off once again to the dark forest, unknowingly to their parents.

Galloping up through the green fields, they decided to go straight to the forest's edge where the little track started.

As they approached the forest, both boys got the strangest feeling not to go in, but the temptation was far too much. When they reached the single file track once again, they didn't pause for a minute, they just kept riding on at a steady trot into the eerie darkness of the mysterious forest.

They both became a little nervous as they rode on — the quietness and the stillness of the place was spooky! Eventually they noticed the forest starting to clear again. A couple of minutes later, they were on the edge of the great big, cleared circle where nothing seemed to grow!

They walked the horses over to the same spot where they had previously tied them up. They then headed straight for the rocky outcrop, where they again found the little path which led directly to the rock face wall.

William posed the question, "Henry, are you ready to enter?"

"Yes," Henry replied, still a bit hesitant.

They both walked to the rock face, William gingerly placed his hand on the rock again — Instantly, the same flash of lights accompanied by the slight breeze freshening the air, then came the crackling sound again. At that moment, the rock became semi-invisible as before, the boys could see the path continuing on through the other side of the rock. Without any more hesitation, both boys stepped through the opening into what seemed now, a slightly more familiar place. Then silently, the rock wall closed behind them. They both wondered as they looked at each other's faces, that without Rrrr, they may not find their way back — they could be trapped and not be able to return home. Walking on nervously, they tried to remember just where they had met Rrrr, then they heard a familiar raspy little voice saying mischievously, "you're back I see," Rrrr said in his sly tone, "what do you want this time?"

Henry answered. "Can you tell us what this place is, maybe you can show us around?"

Rrrr jumped onto a higher tree branch and menacingly answered, "you have gone through a doorway to another world." He went on telling the boys that they were going to meet all sorts of little beings who dwell there. That this place they thought was a cave, was only the beginning of what some might consider — a mysterious world.

Both boys started to look around, the place seemed eerily different somehow. Everything was where it should be it seemed but was not solid looking like the outside world.

Henry happened to look down at his feet and realised he wasn't quite touching the ground. This meant he was floating! Then he glanced straight over at William's feet, they both realised that they were floating a little off the ground. William instinctively reached out to grab hold of a small tree for fear of floating away exclaiming... "I'm floating, I'm floating, look Will, so are you!"

William just looked with his mouth open saying. "Take hold of something Henry, or we might float away."

Rrrr started to laugh at them saying, "you silly boys you won't float away, let go, I told you things aren't the same here, you'll get used to it. Ha, ha, ha, ha, ha, ha," he teased.

The boys gingerly let go of the small tree which they had hold of realising they were not going to float away after all. "So why aren't we floating away?" asked Henry.

Rrrr replied rather seriously... "I will explain it to you, everybody has a physical and a spiritual body. In the physical world where you live at the moment, you are heavy — gravity is working on you. But in the spirit world, you are weightless because you don't have a heavy body, hence you are light enough to float!" Rrrr continued even more seriously... "Most people are more concerned with their physical life, than a spiritual. In fact, for most people it's not until they pass over or are preparing to pass over, that they realise that they have a spiritual body." Rrrr went on to explain to the boys that when they entered through the rock door, they left their physical bodies just outside the rock face. He started to laugh and asked, "you boys didn't actually think you went through solid rock, did you? Ha, ha, ha," he laughed out loud.

The smell of his bad breath hit them again as they winced and turned away.

Then Henry naively asked, "what are they doing out there? Or perhaps should I say, what are we doing out there?"

Rrrr carried on seriously, "you are here only in your spirit bodies, outside, your physicals are still looking for the entrance!" He smiled and continued… "When you return through the rock face, you will find that you'll be back in your physical bodies instantly — you will also find that you have only been gone a few minutes in earthly time because time is very different here, in fact in a sense, there is no time here!"

The boys looked puzzled, then William asked, "why are we here, or, for what purpose?"

Rrrr answered, "you are both here so that I can show you a glimpse into your futures. The big fella instructed me to do so, he said it is very important for you to know."

"But how can we see the future when it hasn't happened yet?" enquired Henry.

Rrrr rolled his eyes up, then jumped onto yet another branch of the tree thinking to himself, 'why, oh why, don't these physicals ever get it! I suppose I will have to explain it once again.'

Rrrr started to talk, "Listen carefully, it doesn't matter what year you live in, for you that year is now, but for someone else who is living in a different year, the year they're living in is also now for them. For example, for some people it may seem they're living in the future, compared to others that are in what they call the past. You see, it all depends on whether they are looking forward or backward in what they think is time." Rrrr noticed that the boys still looked perplexed, so he continued to explain...

"In Fire Fly Valley, there is a book, a very large book, and each page represents a year. Imagine you were reading the page 1,800, then 1,800 is now for you. On the other hand, if you were on page 1,700, then that would be now for you also. And page 1,800 would appear to be in what you call the future, is that clearer?"

Rrrr burst out laughing when he looked at the boy's faces, as he knew they would probably think he was mad, and that he was playing tricks on them.

Henry then ventured to ask, "if there is no time in Fire Fly Valley, why is there time here?"

Rrrr raised his eyebrows again and tried to explain more simply saying, "time only affects something with a beginning and an end. Look at it this way, a tree starts off as a seed, then grows large and eventually dies and falls over. So that takes what you call time, but when you are in your spirit body, you do not age, you do not die, you just continue on, so there is no need for time because everything stays as it is, do you get it now?"

Rrrr asked cheekily.

Both the boys looked at each other trying hard to work out what Rrrr was talking about.

Henry frowning earnestly asked, "where is Fire Fly Valley?"

Rrrr quickly responded with… "Hmmm — Fire Fly Valley is where the big fella lives! You know, the one with no arms I was telling you about. The valley is a long way away you might say, or you might say, it is very near. It all depends." Rrrr finished with a smile, he then laughed out loud and jumped to yet another branch where he started to do a little dance.

When the rascal spoke again, he asked, "do you boys see anything unusual here?"

"The whole place is unusual!" William answered as he gestured with his hand.

"No, no, no," Rrrr grumbled with frustration, "shut your eyes for a moment boys… Now open them, tell me — what do you see, what's different?"

As the boys turned their heads and looked around, they realised that they were surrounded by dozens and dozens of little fairy-like creatures! Some were going about their business, but most of them were just staring at the boys. Some were sitting on rocks, others were in the trees, and some were just flying about.

"What are they?" Henry asked with curiosity.

"They are the Nature Spirits," said Rrrr proudly. "They live everywhere here, and also in your physical world. For example, when I was sitting on your windowsill — in your bedroom the other evening, there were many others with me at the same time, but you just didn't see them," he laughed out louder than ever.

"What do they do here?" asked William sincerely.

"They look after the life force that everything has, you could consider them to be the big fella's little helpers, ha, ha, ha."

Rrrr danced around with some of the Nature Spirits in front the boys, they all seemed so happy.

CHAPTER 8

"So, who is this big fella and when are we going to meet him?" Henry impatiently asked.

"He is called, Ugo, he lives in Fire Fly Valley." Rrrr answered.

"How do we get there?" William asked more politely.

"Well," answered Rrrr, "that's the mystery, I know a way," he said with a cunning look on his face, "but you'll have to wait until you meet Ugo, you see he's the Boss! But I can show you something now, something special you can actually see," he finished looking at the boys enquiringly.

"What's that?" asked Henry.

"Well… It's your future, would you like to see it?" Rrrr asked rubbing his dirty hands together.

Both boys looked at each other, then William looked at the Rascal and answered, "Yes, yes we would."

Rrrr started to grin, because he knew they would both be startled — to say the least.

"All right then, who wants to go first?"

Henry spoke first saying, "I will, I'll go first if that's fine with you Will?" William nodded as he usually took the lead.

"Okay boys, come over here with me." Rrrr led Henry over to a very clear still pool of water and said seriously, "Now I want you to look into this clear pool of water and tell me what you see?"

At first Henry could only see his reflection and said, "I see myself, that's all!"

"Be patient, keep looking, after a few moments you will start to see your future." Rrrr eye's widened, in anticipation.

Henry continued to look into the pond again. Suddenly, he realised he saw himself on a very big ship! it was as though he was looking through someone else's eyes, but he understood it was himself in the future as Rrrr had said.

He was amazed as he looked at himself on the deck. He watched various crew, going about their special duties like setting the rigging and the sails, all seemed busy going about their duties.

As he stood there, he realised he was a fully-grown man wearing a special uniform. He was dressed in snug fitting white trousers, over which hung a long red coat. A fancy sword hung in its scabbard to one side of his hip. He also noticed he was wearing shiny black boots and a fluffy white shirt with cuffs, it seemed he had a particular position on the ship. He also noted he was wearing a three-cornered hat, it was decorated with gold braid around the edges. A telescope was in his left hand, he brought it up to his eye and started to scan the horizon. Some moments later as he spied through his 'glass' — he realised the ship was a full-sized slave trader they had been following, it was getting closer and closer. 'We are gaining on her,' he thought to himself.

A deep voice bellowed from the body Henry now found himself in, it shouted an order…

"Roll out the cannons men, as quickly as you can." Calling to the first officer, he said loudly, "we will be coming about for a broadside, let loose some more sails, so we can gain a little more speed".

This captain, whom Henry seemed to be, looked about again through his telescope, and saw the other ship was now almost running parallel, all its cannons were already run out and exposed.

"Fire a ranging shot," Henry ordered — a moment later there was a loud explosion, a flash of fire shot out from the first canon, then a cannonball could be seen splashing into the sea just short of the slave trader. "Raise the elevation 2° and prepare to fire all cannons," ordered Henry.

Men were running in all directions, a moment later Henry shouted out, "fire."

There was an enormous explosion as flames spat outwards from each Canon, the pungent smell of burnt gunpowder filled the air as the ship healed from the recoil.

Henry swung his telescope around towards the enemy watching carefully and checking how much destruction had occurred on the trader, he could see most of the rigging had started to fall, some sails were down, the remainder now had many holes blasted straight through them.

Men could be seen running and scrambling, a moment later a row of fiery tongues could be seen from the slave traders' cannons, then came the massive explosion of cannonballs striking Henry's beloved ship, the 'Provident'.

Henry shouted again. "Fire when ready men." This time the recoil was a little less extreme as the canons fired off one by one, black smoke was everywhere, and the pungent smell of gunpowder again filled the air. Henry raised his telescope to see if he had finally put a stop to the enemies' attack.

A slight smile appeared at the corner of Henry's mouth as he called to the first officer,

"I think we have the situation under control, prepare the crew for boarding."

Two hours later, Henry had the enemy locked up, then he placed a small crew from the Provident, on board the enemy vessel, so that she could be sailed back to port.

Eventually Henry knew she would be repaired and renamed and then put back into service again.

Henry walked along the deck inspecting the damage that the slave trader had inflicted, he also went downstairs and congratulated the powder boys with their black faces and the look of exhaustion they now carried, without their help he thought, winning the battle would not have been possible.

The Powder boys' job had been to carry gunpowder to each cannon, the boys would run bare footed from the hull of the ship where the gunpowder was stored carrying two leather pouches full of powder. The pouches were heavy and the deck usually wet, running past open gun ports made them an easy target for a sharpshooter on an enemy vessel, usually no more than fifty meters away in battle, so many boys were lost.

The boys were used because adults were too big for the confined spaces between the lower decks.

Rrrr suddenly broke Henry's spell when he asked, "have you had enough Henry?"

Suddenly Henry realised he was a boy again looking into a pool of water. He lifted his head as he asked Rrrr, "what was all that about, I don't understand?"

Rrrr chuckled, "that was you, Henry. In your future — you will be a captain of a 'Man of War', your job is to stop slavery, the ship you just took was a slave trader."

Henry was speechless, his mouth dropped open as he slowly realised, then asked Rrrr.

"I don't understand how I can be here, and yet I can be there also at the same time?"

Rrrr answered, "all we really did just now, is have a look in the book of life a few pages ahead, or in your case, a few years ahead, it's easy for us."

Rrrr then turned to William and asked, "what about you William, are you ready to have a look?"

William gingerly walked over to the little pond where he was asked to look in as Henry had. First of all, he also only saw himself, then suddenly he found himself inside an adult body.

He was in a very big, impressive government building. Above the enormousness front carved wooden doors, there was a large, engraved crest of what appeared to be a king and a shield of some sort. Looking out in front of him, he saw many men sitting and listening to what he was saying… He apparently was giving a speech about abolishing slavery. He listened to himself speaking saying, "we must stop the slavery trade, it's not good, we have to make new laws because innocent people are dying."

He was arguing with other men, some were agreeing with him, but others were not.

There was a vote, many men didn't agree that slavery should be stopped, they wanted it to go on because so much money was being made from the 'slaves' who were forced to work for nothing, but their meagre keep.

William felt very frustrated knowing that for the moment, he was unable to have the laws changed, but he knew that he had to keep trying until new laws were made.

Rrrr spoke, "Have you seen enough William?" He asked.

It was like coming back from a dream, somehow being a young boy here and now, just didn't seem important any more — and he knew it. Rrrr spoke again, "I don't want you coming here for a while, boys, until I organise for you to meet the big fella. I will let you know when because I'm always near you." He chuckled mischievously. "I will show you the way back now, come on boys follow me." Rrrr led the way.

Again, the little path that had mysteriously disappeared, suddenly reappeared, as Rrrr led the way towards the rock face again.

William and Henry walked along the little path following Rrrr. They both realised that the path appeared just a meter or two in front of them. Behind them, the path just as mysteriously disappeared! It was like the path was only there, where they were treading — 'very strange,' they thought to themselves.

CHAPTER 9

Several weeks past, both William and Henry had been restricted to riding around the manor grounds because they were waiting for Rrrr to contact them so they could go and meet UGO.

In the meantime, Eli their father, was due for promotion from Captain to Vice-Admiral. There was to be a lot of pomp and ceremony; The promotion was being held on his ship which was moored in the beautiful port of Willington. Hundreds of guests were expected, and of course Elizabeth, the boys and her now ageing father would all be there.

The years leading up to Eli's promotion had been daunted with constant skirmishes between slave traders and the navy. Slave traders were doing everything possible to stay in their lucrative business, while the Navy was constantly trying to prevent them from continuing their dastardly acts.

On the day of Eli's promotion to Vice-Admiral, everybody of any important status was there, all were dressed in their dress uniforms, shiny boots, complimented with shiny razor-sharp swords! The ladies were also dressed in fine gowns, wearing beautiful hats decorated with plumes of all different colours. Of course, an abundance of jewellery was being flaunted. Elizabeth was dressed more modestly, and very tastefully. The boys were wearing duplicate, coloured suits, looking a little like toy soldiers themselves, everybody was dressed for the occasion, and all seemed very joyous.

Eli's ship the White Eagle, was a double decker which had triple masts. A beautiful gold-gilded carved maiden, hung below the massive bow sprit. She was a heavily armed vessel, but for today's presentation, some of the crew and most of the heavy cannons had been removed for maintenance, leaving only one usable canon.

Everything was made shipshape and tidy, sails rolled perfectly, decks were scrubbed, and the remaining sailors were also all in uniform. The weather was perfect with only a slight breeze, everything appeared to be going as planned.

Unknowingly to the Captain and the Navy officers, a spy had been lingering around the wharves and the local pubs for several weeks, talking to the sailors. He was a sailor himself, as a result he got along well with the other sailors.

The spy had worked diligently, he found out about the plans for Eli's coming promotion, the date, and the fact that the 'White Eagle' would be virtually unarmed.

The spy worked for Captain Black, who was a

vicious character. He wore a scar right down his left cheek, it had been given to him by another captain from another slave trader. Black had been nicknamed Captain Darkness due to his ruthless attitude towards slaves. Captain Black wanted to cripple the White Eagle, as he knew the White Eagle was one of the fastest Navy ships in the sea, he also knew if she was sunk at the wharf, the ship would be out of action, and the wharf rendered useless, as no ship would be able to tie up there.

His plan was to wait until the ceremony was in full swing, then sail into the harbour under a friendly flag, surprise the Navy, and hopefully sink the White Eagle while she lay moored. Thanks to his spy, he knew she had very few armaments on board, a successful attack also meant the killing of many top Navy officers. He sniggered to himself, 'this is going to be easy, we'll sink the White Eagle and then we'll celebrate.'

On the day of the ceremony, most of the officers were on board the White Eagle accompanied by their wives. There was a large band playing on the wharf, everybody's attention was taken up with the ceremony.

Nobody seemed noticed or take care, when a medium-size cutter was spotted flying a friendly flag. She came cruising around the head land and slowly sailed into the bay.

The few people that did notice her thought she was part of the celebration, and so took no notice of the approaching vessel.

The cutter was a medium-sized Eastern trader, she was fast but not heavily armed because on this occasion, she didn't need to be. Captain Black thought he had made a very clever plan, it seemed all was going well. He had been lucky enough to have acquired a senior officer from another vessel, who came with great recommendations. The new officer had trained up his crew very well, and Black was very pleased with his gunners' accuracy.

The plan was to sail up close flying a friendly flag, and then turn hard to run parallel with the White Eagle as she lay moored. With his eight guns all readied, it was just a matter of firing one by one as he passed the moored White Eagle, 'devastation was assured,' he thought to himself. After the attack he intended to sail straight out of the bay before anyone could do anything to stop him.

Unknowingly to him, Ugo was the new officer who had trained the gun crew aboard the Eastern trader. Ugo had been watching everything and knew exactly what the plan was, but Ugo also had a plan.

As the Eastern trader came closer and closer, the first officer from the White Eagle took up a telescope for closer inspection of the approaching vessel — a puzzled look fell on his face as he said to one of the other officers, "she doesn't look like one of ours, and she's getting very close."

At that moment, the cutter started to turn showing her side. The first officer suddenly realised her eight-gun ports were all open, she had begun to roll out her eight canons and was preparing for a broadside. The first officer shouted to the other officers, "we are under attack men," but by that time, the cutter was in a broadside position.

The order had been given by the Eastern trader's Captain Black, for his gun crew to fire at their leisure. Ugo, who was in charge of the gunnery attack on board the Eastern trader, carefully calculated the elevation, so that the canons would miss their target and fire short, or over the White Eagle. He knew it might mean the destruction of some of their sails and rigging, he also knew that some of the crew could be hurt or even killed, but he had to make everything look authentic.

The captain of the cutter didn't have any naval experience, with Ugo's help most of the cannon balls actually missed the White Eagle altogether — others just tore through the sails and the rigging, instead of hitting the hull which would have sunk the white Eagle.

On the White Eagle, there was very little the crew could do, as they had limited canons and hardly any cannon balls — however, Ugo was watching and continued on with his plan.

Ugo, still dressed like a sailor on the trader, just rose upwards, and suddenly out of nowhere, appeared on the deck of the White Eagle!

Henry and William had been standing back in the crowd, watching the ceremony when the attack started and were very near to where Ugo intended to appear. Suddenly, right in front of the boys, a sailor appeared and took the boys by the hand saying, "quickly boys, come with me — I need your help." Henry and William followed him instantly without question.

"Hurry," he said, "follow me to the powder room." When all three arrived Ugo said, "take these two leather bags and fill them with gunpowder over there, from the casks."

Both William and Henry took a bag each and filled them up with powder.

Ugo then said hastily, "quick boys, follow me up to the gunnery deck." Ugo had to lead the way but was too big for the confines of the lower deck. He hoped the boys wouldn't notice when he made himself as small as they were in order to get through the decks! The passageway was low, but for young boys it was easy following Ugo, who was by now well ahead. They ran along the slippery lower deck, then clambered up a small gangway, which led to where the one solitary canon stood, like a guard staring out to sea.

To their amazement, Ugo was already there, appearing full-sized again! Just for a moment, William wondered how he got through the low decks, but there was no time for thinking.

Henry immediately knew what to do, he had watched the powder boys many times before when he had been a captain — albeit in the future. Henry ran with the powder to the cannon, Ugo had already sponged the barrel in preparation. Taking the powder from Henry, he rammed it hard down the barrel — followed by the cannon ball. Once done, all three of them carefully rolled the big cannon out and tightened up the recoil ropes. Ugo seemingly from nowhere, produced a candle to light up the powder and said…

"One muzzle, one shot, we will aim it to hit the cutters helm, so her steering will be rendered useless then she'll drift over to the rocks where she can be boarded."

Ugo thought to himself. 'Eli will capture another 'kingpin' of the slave trading,' "Good," said Ugo, "she's ready to go, don't worry boys, I will make sure the ball hits the helm, just wait a little longer."

Captain Black on the cutter, had been very annoyed to see most of his cannon balls were aimed too high, or missed their target altogether. He had his suspicions about who was responsible for such a bad error — 'the new gunnery officer,' he thought to himself.

Captain Black decided to steer the cutter in a big circle, making it possible to come around for another attack — shouting to his crewmen... "Prepare for another broadside men; roll out the eight canons, be ready to fire on my command and this time don't miss!" He bellowed.

Ugo stood there by the single canon, ready for the cutter to line up. Then he told the boys, "When the cutter starts to make her second pass, we have to fire before she does — so are you ready boys?"

"Yes sir, we are ready," they answered excitedly in unison.

"Just a little longer now, a little longer." The boys were awaiting his final order — when Ugo shouted...

"Now boys — quickly light her up. Henry, put your hands over your ears and stand back boys."

There was an almighty loud explosion as the canon reeled backwards and a flame shot out from its muzzle. All three watched as the ball perfectly made its mark. It hit the helm sending two helmsmen into the next world!

As Ugo had predicted, the cutter suddenly lost direction and started to head towards the rocks. She fired off her cannons, but all missed their target, most balls just landing in the water.

The cutter was now out of control, it headed for the rocks just beyond the wharf, moments later she came to an abrupt halt crashing against sharp rocks.

By that time, the rock wall was swarming with Navy guards toting long rifles, there was no chance for the crew of the slave trader to escape. At the same time, a sailor who had been avoiding his duties, was drinking rum below decks. He had watched all of this unfold — he had watched the boys running all three of them, then to his amazement, one had suddenly grown into a full-size man! The sailor had been far too scared to move, shaking with fear and still holding his now half full tank of rum, he stayed crouched looking. He watched as the two boys scurried up the gangway. The sailor standing by the cannon, he didn't recognise. Suddenly he turned into a semi-transparent giant bottle with no arms or legs! Then, without warning, it just disappeared! The sailor dropped his tank of half spilt rum and ran, thinking to himself, 'I'm never drinking again.'

CHAPTER 10

Elizabeth fortunately was not one of the victims, although she was left standing with blood spatters on her beautiful dress from another less fortunate lady, who'd been severely hurt by a piece of rigging that had fallen from above.

Eli was beside Elizabeth, his arm protectively around her, whilst she was saying frantically…

"We must find the boys, Eli, we must find them."

Eli assured her saying, "I have alerted my men, they're already out looking for the boys. We will find them dear, don't worry so." Eli said trying to comfort Elizabeth.

Just then the first mate ran across the now wet slippery deck to Eli calling out…

"Sir, sir, we have found your boys, they are safe and unharmed — they were with a sailor when the attack happened, he seemed to have taken care of them sir."

"Where's the boys now?" Eli asked, "where are they, I must see them and also this sailor."

Next thing, the boatswain and a petty officer appeared with the boys in tow, immediately the boys saw Eli and Elizabeth, they let go of the officer's hands and ran over to their parents. All four were smiling with relief, as Ugo looked on from nearby chuckling to himself.

Eli thanked the officers. Just for a moment everything seemed calm and normal, but it wasn't.

"Where were you boys?" Elizabeth questioned. "We got separated — what happened?"

The boys told them the story about the sailor coming and helping them prime and fire the one working canon that was on board, they spoke about how the sailor seemed to direct the canon ball straight at the helm. "A dead accurate shot!" William said proudly.

Eli asked, "where is this sailor? I want to meet him."

"I don't know," said William, "we left him standing by the cannon after it was all over, then the boatswain and the first mate brought us to you."

"I must find him, and thank him, he deserves a medal!" Eli insisted. Later on, that afternoon, when Eli and the first officer sat down, they discussed what had happened and why?

All in all, three sailors had lost their lives, the rest of the injuries were minor, two ladies were badly injured unfortunately.

The lesson that came from this event, was that all captains at all times must be ready and not be complacent.

The good thing that came out of all this, was the

captain, a ringleader from the slave trade, was now in chains with the rest of his crew.

That night when everything had settled down, peace seemed to rein over the manner once more. The next day Eli spoke to the boys, he was trying to find out more information about this elusive sailor, who had managed to save so many lives and was also responsible for capturing the complete crew of the invading ship.

He said to the boys at breakfast, "we have to find that sailor, you're the only ones who can recognise him boys."

The following day, Eli was at the wharf on his ship trying to figure out how this elusive sailor, who didn't seem to belong to his crew, managed to get aboard and take charge of the one and only working Canon.

"He has to be found," he said to the first officer, "we must find this man."

The first officer made it his priority asking all the crew if anybody had seen what had happened, and if they knew who this sailor might have been. But no one knew anything!

A few days later, Eli had all the crew lined up, the two boys were told to come and inspect them to see if the crew member that helped them was there. The boys looked at every sailor checking them thoroughly, but both came back to their father saying, "No, Dad, he's not there."

That night when William and Henry were lying in their bed thinking about the excitement they'd had that day, how they and their sailor friend managed to send the other ship onto the rocks, it had all been so exciting and a bit scary. They then both heard a little laugh. "Ha ha-ha-ha," there was Rascal perched on the windowsill again saying… "You'll never find that sailor unless I tell you who it was."

Henry quickly sat up asking, "you rascal, who was he? You must tell us."

"I think it was the big fella," he provoked.

"I thought you said he looked like a bottle?" said William.

"He can take any shape he wants," answered Rrrr, "no one else could have known, that you Henry, would know how to prime a cannon. Also, no one else could have possibly known, how to direct the canon ball to exactly the right target, it had to be him."

"Well dad wants to meet him to thank him, he wants to give him a medal."

Rrrr laughed out loud nearly falling off the windowsill! "I'm not sure if he would want to meet Eli, however, I'll ask him when I next see him. As far as the medal goes, he doesn't want or need a medal." The Rascal laughed again saying… "You boys did very well, you saved a lot of people's lives, also you helped capture a bad slave trader. I'm going to arrange for you both to meet the big fella Ugo, very soon. I'll let you know when and where of course." After saying that, Rascal leapt out of the window. The boys could hear him laughing in the distance, as he disappeared into a misty cloud.

CHAPTER 11

William and Henry had been talking about whether they should tell their parents about Ugo, and how he appeared as a sailor and saved the White Eagle and many people from dying.

The problem was, they would also have to tell them about the forest and the cave, or should I say the entrance to the other world. It was quite a dilemma for the boys.

Unknowingly to them, had they told their mum she would have understood anyway, because she came from the other world.

Some days later, Rrrr appeared to Elizabeth, she hadn't seen him for quite some time, but felt he was often lingering nearby.

She didn't like Rrrr very much as she knew he was mischievous and could cause problems as he had in the past.

"What do you want Rrrr?" she asked a little annoyed.

"I've come to tell you who fired the cannon ball at the slave trader's cutter — do you want to know?" He asked in a sly provocative way.

"Yes, of course I want to know Rrrr...also Eli wants to give this sailor a medal."

At that, Rrrr couldn't contain himself and erupted in laughter... "Ha, ha, ha, ha, that's so funny," he rebuked Elizabeth but continued... "Ugo doesn't want a medal, what's the use of that? Also, Elizabeth, Ugo doesn't want you to know that I've been meeting with the boys."

Elizabeth's face went red, 'Ugo,' she thought, 'that makes more sense.' She became angry, she didn't want the boys to know about any of this, Fire Fly Valley, THE DOOR, Ugo and Jack, or about her true identity.

"What have you told them?" She demanded.

"I haven't told them anything," a sly grin came over rascal's face as one of his ears started to twitch!

"Isn't it enough that because of me — Ugo saved the ship. I haven't told them anything about you, and I won't because the big fella told me not to, no slip of the tongue Ugo said, everything has to be a big secret, no gossiping," he smugly said.

"Tell me, how do the boys know about you?"

"Well, I met them in the forest," Rrrr admitted.

"But they're not allowed to go to the forest!" Elizabeth exclaimed.

"I know," answered Rrrr with a cunning smirk.

"What's in that forest? Tell me, I want to know," demanded Elizabeth.

Rrrr started to look sheepish and looked around to escape her gaze. He became agitated and jumped up on the windowsill in case he had to make a quick escape.

"Well, in the forest there's an entrance, a back door if you like to visit Fire Fly Valley."

He kept looking away to avoid her gaze, and to make sure she wasn't going to do something horrible to him.

"You mean there's another entrance to Fire Fly Valley?" asked Elizabeth incredulously.

"Yes, yes," continued Rrrr, "sometimes the big fella comes through there, and we chat."

"You have to tell me everything you rascal — that you've told the boys about Fire Fly Valley. They have to be guided, not thrown into the deep end! They just cannot be allowed to find things out on their own." She finished sounding a little irritated.

"I know, I know," Rrrr replied quickly trying to explain... "When you saw Ugo and Jack the last time Elizabeth, they both wanted to meet the boys properly, but obviously they couldn't — but since then I have intervened just a little," he winced looking straight at Elizabeth, "Ugo and Jack are now able to come and meet the boys, so you should be happy about that Elizabeth, you can come with them now." He said hopefully.

Elizabeth calmed down a little, she knew sooner or later the boys were going to find out about Ugo anyway, Jack and maybe even me, she thought to herself.

The twin boys, Henry and William had just turned thirteen. 'It seems they are growing into young men already,' Elizabeth thought to herself.

Time passed slowly for Elizabeth, she felt she hadn't heard from Rrrr for quite some time as she was still waiting for the meeting with Ugo and Jack in the forest. She wondered to herself why Ugo had never mentioned there was a back door so close to the manor. 'All these years,' she thought, 'I could have gone back to see how Andi was doing, or to see my Uncle Jack, it all seems a bit strange,' she mused.

Eli and Elizabeth were relaxing in the gazebo, it had been a beautiful summer's night, the moon was bright to the point the trees in the garden were casting shadows. They had been playing cards and were sitting opposite each other. Behind Eli, something caught Elizabeth's eye. There swinging from the corner of the gazebo was Rrrr — he was frantically signalling her, holding a finger over his mouth.

"Elizabeth, don't let on I'm here," came a voice in Elizabeth's head, Rrrr went on, "you must ride to the forest with the boys to meet Ugo and Jack tomorrow Elizabeth."

Then without warning he leapt from the gazebo back into the darkness. 'That rascal,' thought Elizabeth. 'He caught me by surprise, I nearly called out his name.'

"Did you say something dear?" Eli asked as he placed his last card on the table.

"No, no darling, I was just thinking how nice it would be for me to go riding with the boys, tomorrow. I'd like to surprise them, what do you think Eli?"

Eli thought for a moment, it was a bit unusual for

Elizabeth to go riding with the boys but,

"Well dear, it sounds like a good idea, you haven't been riding in a long while, and you could all take a picnic lunch, that would be nice? Anyway, I have to go to the White Eagle to make sure the new captain has got everything under control. Also, as you know, since being made Vice Admiral, I have less and less time to be with you or the boys, so go ahead and enjoy yourselves," he finished off.

CHAPTER 12

The next morning while the family were having breakfast, Elizabeth said to William and Henry... "Boys, I would like to come riding with you today, we could take a picnic lunch, what do you say boys?" She tried to stay calm and relaxed as she glanced over the table at them.

Both boys looked at each other and William said, "Yes, yes mother, that would be very nice."

William thought to himself, 'now what are we going to do? Rrrr asked us to go to the forest.'

Henry later on said to William, "You know don't you that Rrrr wants us to meet him today in the forest? What are we going to do now that Mom wants to come Will?"

"I'm not sure... we can't upset mother if she wants to come riding with us, so that's what we'll have to do go riding, then have our picnic and be good little boys!"

An hour later, all three were saddled up and ready to go — they cantered off gently riding through the long green grass. Eventually, they came to the end of the manor grounds and in the distance the dark mysterious forest could be seen. The boys took no notice on purpose.

Suddenly Elizabeth said, "shall we ride to the forest boys?" Both William and Henry felt a little shocked as they looked around at their mother, both had a surprised look on their faces. William spoke first exclaiming... "But we are not allowed mom!"

"It's all right," Elizabeth said, "if you're with an adult, it will be fine... so come on boys, let's go!" she said urging her horse onwards.

They all started to ride at a nice slow canter, Henry leading the way. Elizabeth didn't really know what to expect, she just knew that sooner or later she would meet up with Rrrr, Ugo and hopefully Jack.

As they cantered towards the forest the horses headed directly to where the small path started as they were now used to going there. At the edge of the forest, there in front of Elizabeth and the boys, started the little path. Elizabeth turned to the boys and said, "There's no need to play any more games boys, I know you have been here before, so Henry, lead the way please." The boys didn't know what to say, they just did as they were told.

Henry led the way, followed by William and then Elizabeth, they slowly walked along the little single file path which headed deep into the forest. As they went on, Elizabeth was wondering if the boys really knew where to go. Sometime later, Elizabeth called out to the boys... "Do you do know where you're going boys?"

"Yes Mother," replied Henry, "it won't be long now."

The darkness that had encompassed them during the ride through the forest, now started to lift, all three were able to see more sunshine ahead. A few moments later, they were on the edge of the enormous clearing. The boys stopped and turned to their mother saying, "this is it, this is where we found 'The Door.' This is where we met Rrrr."

Elizabeth then said, "I already know about your little friend, the rascal, so you better tell me everything I think!"

The boys glanced at each other wondering how she knew all this. Henry decided it was better to tell her everything, so they explained all about the rock face, the nature spirits, Rrrr, and the future pond.

"Let's tie the horses up," Elizabeth said, 'then you can both show me." After securing Bonnie and Bobby, there was no need to search for the rock face, by now they knew exactly where to go. It took no time at all to get to the rocky outcrop with Henry eagerly leading the way. They all followed the path that led directly to the rock face stopping in front of the big rock. All three just stood there gazing at it! Elizabeth spoke.

"What's going on, this path ends here, are you boys playing games with me?"

"No, no," William spoke out, "look Mom, when I place my hand on the rock here, some sort of magic happens, and an access point appears. Then we can go through, it's okay Mom, are we allowed, and do you want to do it with us?" He asked all three questions at once.

Elizabeth trying to be and sound in control said, "show me, show me what you do." William placed his hand on the rock, a moment later, coloured lights started to flash, a slight breeze arose, there directly in front of all three they could see the entrance.

The boys started to get excited asking permission to go through. "Yes," Elizabeth said, "and I will follow you." Elizabeth had already realised that the opening through the rock resembled THE DOOR but didn't and couldn't say anything about that.

A couple of steps later, all three were through the rock face. The boys turned to their mom and William said. "It's very different and a bit strange here, but it's nice, it's beautiful, this is where we met Rrrr for the first time."

Henry then beckoned… leading the way and telling her about all the nature spirits that lived here, and how it was like another world underground.

Then Henry continued excitedly, "here Mom, come over here and have a look at this pond, we call this the future pond! Rrrr told us to look into the pond so we would be able to see into our futures, it's the strangest thing."

Elizabeth was thinking to herself, 'Rrrr should never have shown them all this without asking me first,' she looked at the boys and gestured to them.

"Sit down over here with me boys, I have something to tell you both."

She proceeded to tell them about knowing Ugo and

Jack, and also all the nature spirits. She also mentioned Fire Fly Valley, and what sort of place it was as best she could. She didn't mention who she really was, as that would be telling them too much. Then she said knowingly, "be prepared boys, we're going to meet someone here very soon, in fact I think they may be here, already."

She was right — three of them, Ugo, Jack, and Rrrr had been listening to what Elizabeth had been telling the boys.

Then, a slight movement in the air occurred, directly in front of them stood Ugo with Jack beside him and sitting on a nearby tree branch was Rrrr!

Ugo came close to Elizabeth who was standing with Henry on one side of her, and William on the other.

The boys just stood there staring in amazement at the huge figure directly in front of them, he had two big eyes, no mouth, no arms! He was quite tall and resembled a great big bottle! As they looked at him, he started to smile then chuckling out loud.

"It's lovely to meet you boys," it said, "I am called Ugo, and this is Jack, my great friend. Rrrr has told me lots of things about you both, we have been looking forward to meeting with you two."

Jack came closer, he greeted the boys individually and told them that he was Elizabeth's uncle. Both boys looked straight up at Elizabeth, wondering how this man could have possibly been her uncle. Elizabeth knew exactly what they were thinking and said to them. "He's not my real uncle, he's a pretend uncle."

Both boys seemed to be more satisfied with this

answer, well, just for the moment.

Rrrr, unusual for him, didn't say anything. He just remained sitting on his branch. Because Ugo was there, Rrrr seemed to have lost his tongue! He was nowhere as cheeky as he normally was.

Ugo came even closer and surrounded the boys and Elizabeth in his beautiful, serene bubble of love. The boys had never experienced anything quite like this before, they didn't understand what was going on really, but they knew everything was fine and they were safe.

Ugo stepped back a little, when both the boys spoke at once asking. "Who are you, what are you?"
Ugo answered, "I'm from Fire Fly Valley, I am here to help you, or anybody else that may need help. My friend Jack is also here for the same reason. I know that Rrrr showed you how to see future events when you look into the pool. Remember when you came under attack on the White Eagle, I was the one who helped you fire the Cannon."

"No, that was a sailor," William said almost indignantly.

"Yes, you are correct," smiled Ugo, "but it was still me, watch," then he instantly turned into the sailor, "recognise me at all?" he asked and laughed. The next moment, he changed back into his large bottle body he preferred to use.

"You see boys, I can take on any shape or form I like, for example, I can be a tree, or a bird, or a house — whatever I want!"

"Are you a magician?" William asked incredulously.

Ugo started to laugh even more, then looked straight at Elizabeth and asked.

"How are you Elizabeth my dear?"

"I'm fine thanks Ugo, it's so good to see you and Uncle Jack again," she went closer towards Jack.

"And how are you uncle?"

"I'm also fine," he said with a wink!

She looked back at Ugo.

"What is this place Ugo? I have never seen it before, I was surprised to find out it's like some sort of backdoor to Fire Fly Valley, as Rrrr suggested."

"Yes, you could call it that, and there are many of them scattered throughout the world."

"Why didn't you tell me Ugo there was one so close by to our home?"

"Because," Ugo explained, "it was never intended for regular use, however, I instructed Rrrr to show the boys a little of their future, because their upcoming jobs are so important to mankind. And in any case, it came in handy for Henry to know what to do when the White Eagle was under attack."

Both the boys had been listening to all of this, they were trying to understand what was going on, when William asked.

"Why are we floating just off the ground?" Elizabeth hadn't noticed it herself as she was more used to such phenomena.

Ugo answered, "I know Rrrr explained it to you before, but I will say again, you are here in your spirit form, your physical bodies are still outside the cave. While we have been in here for several hours, when you step back through the rock wall, you will be instantly returned to your physical bodies, and it is then that you will notice virtually no time will have passed." He chuckled to himself about the word time, what it really meant, or didn't mean, he chuckled again. Ugo went over to Elizabeth and said quietly, "I can't have Eli or your father knowing about this place Elizabeth, or anything about what's going on just yet. You know that don't you? When the boys leave here today and pass through the rock wall, they will start to forget what happened here. By the time they get back to the manor, they will have forgotten everything about this place and will remember nothing about ever coming here to the forest! Jack and I will always be around, to make sure everything is going as planned." Ugo ended saying, "You should all be going now." Rrrr jumped down from the tree branch where he had been sitting all this time. He looked at Elizabeth and the boys and said rather loudly, "follow me."

Elizabeth glanced back and gave a small wave to both Ugo and Jack. Instantly a little path appeared in front of them, Rrrr, Elizabeth and the two boys all drifted along towards the rock face. As they approach the rock face, the opening appeared, Elizabeth and the two boys drifted straight through the rock and were instantly in their physical bodies!

Without any talking, all three walked back to the horses. Indeed, nothing much else was said as they rode through the dark forest following the narrow path, which eventually took them out into the bright sunlight once more.

"Come on boys," Elizabeth called, "I'll race you both to the beginning of the manor grounds."

Elizabeth gently dug her heels into the horses' flanks — almost immediately the horse broke into a gallop with the two boys in hot pursuit.

An hour later, they were gently trotting towards the stables where they dismounted. The stable boy took the reins and led the horses into the stables to be groomed.

Elizabeth and the two boys walked back towards the manor, testing their memory she looked at them and asked, "did you enjoy your ride today boys?"

"Oh yes," they both said in unison. "It was lovely."

Back at the manor Eli was waiting, he greeted them and asked the boys a similar question, "did you all have a good ride today, and where did you go?"

Henry answered, "yes Father, we went right up to the top boundary, then we followed the trail which led along the plateau, it was a great ride."

Elizabeth heard this and thought to herself, 'good, they have no idea about ever going into the forest and meeting Ugo and Jack, or Rrrr,' she took a deep breath and thought to herself, 'Ugo's correct again.'

CHAPTER 13

Eli, now Vice Admiral, was still frustrated trying to find out who the sailor was that saved the White Eagle and many lives, when the attack took place in Willington Harbour.

Rrrr was still lurking around, Elizabeth had seen him a couple of times, and she knew sooner or later he would be up to his old tricks of trying to cause trouble.

It seemed the boys had forgotten all about the dark forest and were now content riding their horses in the manor grounds. Occasionally, they would go with Eli to the harbour when a new Navy 'Man of War' ship was visiting.

They both loved going aboard and being shown around usually by the first officer, it was very interesting as he instructed them about many of the ship's manoeuvrings etc.

Henry already was thinking that one day he would like to be the commander of a 'Man-of-war' — he just knew it somehow.

Unknowing to the boys, Rrrr was almost always nearby observing them. He was supposed to be keeping an eye on them and reporting back to Ugo on their welfare, but Rrrr couldn't help himself, he just had a mischievous mind, and was always thinking to himself, 'hmmm, what can I do next!'

One night when Eli was sleeping, Rrrr entered his dream. Like the interfering rotten little rascal he was, he decided to tell Eli some things that he was not allowed to tell.

Eli had been dreaming about the attack on the White Eagle, when Rrrr's little voice told him that there was a sailor on board who had witnessed the boys carrying gunpowder, on the day of the attack. When Eli awoke the next morning, he couldn't remember whether he had actually been dreaming. But he did have a strong feeling, to interview the crew that were on board the day of the attack.

About a week later, he had the original crew visit his office, which was in a large building overlooking Willington harbour.

One by one he re-interviewed the crew, it seemed he was getting nowhere until one of the sailors broke down and admitted seeing the boys on the fateful day. Eli demanded the sailor to tell the whole truth this time asking…

"Why didn't you tell me this the first time man?" He demanded sharply.

"Sorry sir, it was because I was supposed to be doing deck duties at that time, but I went below to get out of my duties sir."

He started to shake as he knew he was in a lot of trouble and could even be flogged.

Eli was very annoyed with him, but managed to calm down a little, then said to the sailor.

"Tell me everything you know, or you will be put in irons and flogged!"

"Well sir, you'll probably think I'm mad, but I saw the two boys with another sailor who was not of this crew, I don't know how he got there or who he was. But that's not all of it sir."

Now he began visibly trembling as he continued... "I was hiding, I was in the lower decks thinking, 'no one will find me in here drinking the rum!' Then I heard people running, it was the two boys, they were carrying gunpowder to the cannon. This took place not far away from where I was hiding, so I saw it all. The strangest thing was, there was a sailor with them dressed like an adult, but he appeared to be the same size as the boys! Then all three came running past me to get to the above cannon." He looked at Eli, to see if he was taking it all in — strange as it was.

"At that moment, while the two boys were placing their leather satchels down, the sailor suddenly grew into a full-size man! I know it sounds very strange sir, I had to rub my eyes twice and look again wondering what on earth was going on. In fear of being caught I stayed hidden for a while longer. I watched the boys place the gunpowder in the barrel, I then watched the sailor ram it home. Next thing the cannon was fired. I watched closely and heard the sailor tell the boys to go up to the next deck, where the boatswain and a petty officer would be.

"The last I saw of the boys were when they were going up the gang way to the main deck. Then something even more strange happened, the sailor who was standing no more than 10 meters from me, changed shape! He grew taller looking like a big glowing bottle, he had no arms and no mouth and appeared to be shimmering. Honestly sir, that's what I saw...It, or he, was almost transparent, I could see through him! Then all of a sudden, he just vanished! I ran like hell! I was scared for my life! I'm sorry sir, very sorry." The sailor finished pitifully.

Eli then asked harshly, "why didn't you tell me this in the first place?"

"I couldn't sir, I was not at my post, and I knew that you or anybody else would think I was drunk at the time, or worse maybe mad, but I was neither."

"Report to the first officer tomorrow, he will take disciplinary action, you are lucky I don't have you flogged right now, get out." Eli said.

Eli now knew that something very strange had happened that day, but it still seemed like it was a dead end, as he had no idea who the sailor was. 'The crew man must have been very drunk,' he thought.

Back at the manor, that evening Eli was talking to Elizabeth about the strange events of the day, and how the sailor when interviewed, had admitted he had seen this bottle like being who appeared to be helping the boys, and also fired the cannon.

He went on, "I think the sailor must be lying or

completely demented or both!" He almost laughed a little glancing at Elizabeth.

A peculiar look fell onto Elizabeth's face as she listened, Eli knew straight away that what he had just told Elizabeth, there might be more to it than what she was letting on, so he asked. "What is it darling? You look a little pale, have you heard rumours, is there something you're not telling me?" Elizabeth faced flushed confirming her secrecy. She knew she couldn't tell Eli anything, he wouldn't understand. She had to think about what to say and what to tell Eli, and how much. Then she excused herself saying politely...

"I'm a little tired tonight, Eli, would you mind if we continued our discussion tomorrow?"

"Of course, dear, you get some rest, and we'll chat further tomorrow — it's been a long day for both of us."

The following morning the question was put aside as Eli was called out to sail on the White Eagle with the new captain, he would be gone several months. Elizabeth felt relieved.

She took a deep sigh wondering if she could get in contact with Ugo to ask him what he thought she should do.

Suddenly she realised, "I know, where that rascal is, I'll ask him!"

He must've been just there listening to her thoughts and watching her, as only minutes later he appeared sitting in one of the lounge chairs which seemed to be enormous for him, since he was so small.

Rrrr asked, "do you want me to summon Ugo?" Elizabeth thought to herself, 'he's always hanging around watching and listening to me, normally I'd be annoyed.'

"Yes, I think you should, it's very important — Eli is becoming suspicious. I can't understand how he found out there was a witness to the event on the White Eagle during the attack?" Elizabeth said looking straight at Rrrr with suspicion on her face.

'I bet it was the rascal,' she thought to herself, 'he's always causing trouble.'

Rrrr communicated… "I'll be in touch with the big fella as soon as I can," he looked around sheepishly and then said, "I best be going now," then flew out of the window.

It was a couple of days later before Ugo appeared to Elizabeth. "Don't worry, my dear," Ugo said softly to her, "no one can hear me, or see me. So, tell me what's the matter?"

Elizabeth explained it all exclaiming… "I really don't know what to say to him, I don't want to tell lies, I just don't know how he will take it. Should I tell him about you and Jack and Rrrr? Please tell me what to do, and what and how I should tell it to Eli?"

Ugo spoke, "We have to think of a careful plan, we either have to tell him everything or nothing! We can't tell him part of it, or he'll continually ask questions and the truth will have to come out in the end."

Ugo considering went on, "You have achieved what you came back to do, Elizabeth, the two boys, Henry and William, are exceptional, and will play a major part in stopping the slave trade in years to come. I'll have to think about which way is the best way to go with Eli."

Elizabeth's father had not been well, he had been spending most of his time either in bed or at best just in the lounge room. Every day she saw more deterioration in his health, 'one can't expect much more at his age,' she thought.

It was about three weeks after Eli had sailed away on the White Eagle when, one morning Judy came to Elizabeth with the news, she said, "I have just been to check on your father, Elizabeth, I'm sorry to tell you this, unfortunately he has passed away during the night."

Although Elizabeth was terribly upset, she knew he would be passing over soon — she was expecting it. She also knew that her father would be either in the transit world, or on his way to the spirit world, either way, he would now be safe and comfortable. He would also be with his real daughter and would have a full understanding of what had happened and why. In this respect, Elizabeth was able to cope with her loss much more easily.

At the funeral, hundreds of people came to pay their respects to Mr Mont Grove, he was very well-known and very well liked in the local society.

There was no way of getting a message to Eli so, she just had to wait for his return. In the meantime, she still had to work out something with Ugo about what she was going to tell Eli when he returned.

She thought about it for some time, realising that her father would have been very upset had he known that Elizabeth, his real daughter, had passed over. On the other hand, Eli had never met the first Elizabeth, 'he had only met me,' she thought to herself. Maybe it wasn't going to be so difficult to explain to Eli everything, upon his return after all.

End of book 4

Lightning Source UK Ltd.
Milton Keynes UK
UKHW042332230522
403422UK00004B/80